*This book is dedicated to the memory
of my great-aunt Chen Feng-mei.*

WHITE LILY

TING-XING YE

Illustrations by Bernadette Lau

Doubleday Canada

Canadian Cataloguing in Publication Data

Ye, Ting-xing, 1952–
    White lily

ISBN 0-385-25896-8

I. Title.

PS8598.E16E45 2000   jC813'.54   C99-931389-4
PZ7.Y4Wh 2000

Jacket photograph courtesy The Royal Asiatic Society/London
Jacket and text design by Janine Laporte
Printed and bound in Canada

Published in Canada by
Doubleday Canada, a division of
Random House of Canada Limited

FRI 10   9   8   7   6   5   4   3   2   1

Nearly a century ago, deep in the center of the Forbidden City, China's last emperor reigned from his dragon throne. Although he was only a boy, the imperial decrees issued in his name were shouted in every corner of the country, binding his subjects with the stout bonds of custom and law, taxes and tribute, rules and regulations. Every man was required to shave his head, leaving a single pigtail to grow from the crown down his back, symbolizing his submission to the boy-emperor. And every woman was second in importance, even in her own family, for the burdens of law and tradition weighed much more heavily on females. They were called to obey their fathers and brothers as young girls, to comply with their husbands after their arranged marriages, and to yield to their sons if they were widowed.

Into this world, one day, in a village in the lower reaches of the Yangtze River, a baby girl was born.

1

L ee Family Village was no ordinary place.
As far as the eye could see, jade-green rice
paddies dotted a land crisscrossed with canals.
The many quiet ponds were home to the most
beautiful lilies in the nation. When in full blossom,
they bathed the air with their sweet fragrance.

Nor was the newborn an ordinary girl. Her
father, Master Lee, was the wealthiest man in the
area, and his family the most prominent. As if to
prove her worthiness to belong to such a clan, the
baby cried out so lustily that she silenced the
cicadas droning rhythmically in the trees, com-
plaining *far too hot! far too hot!* Her shrill wails
brought the villagers rushing to the gates of Master
Lee's house, each anxious to be the first to extend
his congratulations and best wishes.

The richest merchant arrived first, followed by
his wife and household. Next came Master Lee's
tenant farmers, slapping dust from their tattered

trousers with their straw hats as they hurried along. Far behind waddled the local scholar, encircled by a flock of students.

"May I have the honor to make a proposal, noble Sir?" intoned the merchant when all had assembled. "I request that your beautiful child be promised in marriage to my Number One son, who is five years her senior." He held out a red silk pouch filled with silver coins.

With the heavy pouch resting in his palm, Master Lee responded, "I accept this proposition, Sir, and from now on we are relatives."

The crowd cheered the announcement as the head farmer stood out and made a deep bow. "Distinguished Master, we wish your precious girl good health, long life, and all the happiness in the world. May her daughterly obedience and virtue last as long as the universe!"

Behind him, the farmers pressed forward. Hens cuddled under their arms, strings of wriggling fish dangled from their hands, and fresh vegetables and fruit piled on pans were suspended from their shoulder poles. A group of ducks scurried worriedly to and fro under the watchful eyes of a pair of white geese. All this the farmers offered as gifts to the family.

Master Lee accepted the tributes with a silent nod.

"In my humble opinion, respected Lord," wheezed the scholar, puffing from his walk, "your baby girl is the purest among the pure and the finest among the best, like this precious flower." He presented a single, long-stemmed lily in full, white bloom. "May I suggest she be named White Lily?"

"Then White Lily she shall be," Master Lee declared, barely concealing his disappointment that the newborn was not a boy.

2

White Lily was a happy child. She began giggling before she could stand up, and she learned to laugh, louder than her cries, before she was able to wriggle her chubby toes and walk on her own. But her happiest times were those when she pulled off her socks and scampered barefoot across the wooden floors, or outside in the courtyard where the spring sun warmed the cool flagstones. There she played with her elder brother, Fu-gui, and chased after sparrows. However, her running and jumping and shrieks of delight often earned Grandmother's — Nai-nai's — angry scolding, Father's frowns and grumbles, or Mother's gentle criticism for disrupting the household peace.

White Lily was sure that it was not her beating feet that displeased Nai-nai and upset her father, because for as long as she could remember the thump of feet was a familiar noise in their house. It came from Mother and Nai-nai.

WHITE LILY

In White Lily's eyes, the difference between these two important women in her life was as wide as the sky. While Nai-nai was short and chubby, almost balloon-shaped, Mother was tall and slim, much like the lily stems that stood in the ponds. Mother spoke in a soft, quiet manner that would hardly startle a bird, but Nai-nai's voice was loud and firm, as if a brass gong had been struck with a wooden mallet. Mother wore either a long skirt or a full-length robe, often in colorful prints. When she walked, her hips swung rhythmically while her pointed shoe-tips peeped in and out from under the hem. Yet Nai-nai seemed to know one color and one style only. She had chosen to wear black ever since Grandpa had passed away two years before White Lily was born. Her shapeless pants were wide and loose around the hips but narrow at the legs, wrapped tightly at her ankles with black ribbons.

But there was one thing that Mother and Nai-nai had in common — their feet. They were almost as small as White Lily's. Mother's and Nai-nai's richly embroidered silk shoes were even shorter than their own outstretched hands. *How could that be possible?* White Lily wondered, looking down at her own plump feet, which seemed to grow with every passing breeze.

5

Besides, Mother's and Nai-nai's tiny feet were always wrapped in heavy cotton strips. The only time White Lily saw them unveiled was during the "feet-bathing" time at the end of each day, after the household hubbub had died down. Mother would carefully unwind the cloth from Nai-nai's feet, which gave off a sharp and unpleasant odor in warm weather. Nai-nai would then soak her feet in a wooden basin of warm water. She often let out a long and weary sigh, so soft yet anguished that to White Lily she didn't sound like Grandmother at all. Following the same routine, Mother tended to her own feet, but with one exception. In her basin, the water was scented with blossoms or lily petals that floated around her ankles.

"My feet are called Three-Inch Golden Lilies," Nai-nai proudly told White Lily one night. "And I have called them that since I was a little girl." But White Lily didn't understand how such smelly, twisted, and wrinkled knobs could be compared to flowers. On another occasion, when Nai-nai was not around, Mother said bitterly, "These horrible, deformed things are no lilies, my dear daughter, nor are they of gold. They are teardrops. They are even shaped like teardrops. They have caused so many tears that no lily pond is large enough to contain them."

White Lily thought long and hard about the mystery. How could Nai-nai be proud of her shrunken, knobby feet when Mother seemed to hate her own? Usually she would have asked her brother for help, because he was older and smarter since he was attending school. But how could Fu-gui know the answer if he had never laid eyes on a woman's bare feet? Everyone knew that it was strictly against tradition for a man to be present during women's "feet-bathing" time.

White Lily concluded that she would not find out whether the tiny feet were lilies or teardrops unless she was able to go to school and learn to read and write like her brother.

But Mother had told her earlier that for girls, schooling was forbidden.

3

O n the eve of the Chinese New Year, it snowed, a rare occurrence in that part of China. Fat flakes descended from a quiet, black sky, unfolding a thin, white blanket across the village. "This snowfall means good luck," proclaimed White Lily's father. "It will surely bring us another year of prosperity, bumper harvests, joy, and happiness."

When White Lily looked out her window the next morning, snow as thick and wet as cream capped the curved walls of the courtyard and plopped to the flagstones from the bare branches of the willow tree outside her bedroom. She bounded from her bed, threw on her clothes, and ran outside. Everywhere she went, she left behind a track of melting footprints like those of a giant.

Since it was New Year, White Lily was a year older. "You are six now," Mother said to her after breakfast.

"But Brother Fu-gui said that I was born four years, seven months, and eight days ago, and he also said that I am still a child." White Lily raised up her fingers: first four, then seven, then eight. "He is wrong, isn't he?"

To White Lily's big disappointment, Mother failed to notice her new counting skill. "Fu-gui is right. But custom says that you turn six today," her mother replied. "Some traditions don't make sense, and this is one of them," she continued. "On the day you were born, the tenth of July, you were considered to be one year old. Seven months later, when the New Year arrived, you became a year older like everyone else, so you turned two. But in fact —"

"In fact," White Lily interrupted, "I was only seven months old."

Mother responded with a weak smile. "And he's also right that you're still a little girl."

"But that's not what Father said. He is going to let me sit with the rest of the family and the guests at the New Year dinner tonight. You told me last year that it is a treat only for grown-ups," White Lily said cheerfully as she pictured herself seated at the grand, vermilion-painted table. It was an event that she had been awaiting for years.

Many times in the past she had sneaked into the storage room in which the huge tabletop leaned against the wall, a dustcover draped over it. On each occasion, White Lily would lift the corner of the drapery and stroke the glossy surface of the table with her palm, or admire her own reflection. She was sure that the perfect, round tabletop was even wider than the lily pond at the back of the courtyard; and she was equally certain that from now on she would be happy because she was no longer a child.

During the meal, as servants scooted to and fro with plates of savory stewed chicken, roast duck, steamed fish, stir-fried vegetables, and heaping bowls of rice, she even escaped the usual warnings from Nai-nai and her father not to eat and talk at the same time.

No one can sit still on occasions like this, surrounded by so many people and so much delicious food, White Lily assured herself. Across the table, her father, Nai-nai, the merchant and his wife — her future father- and mother-in-law — chatted and laughed as they plied their chopsticks and tipped their wine cups.

But something was wrong with her mother, White Lily noticed. All through the meal — no, all through the day, she recalled — Mother had been unusually quiet. Now she seemed sad.

"Is Mother ill?" White Lily whispered to Fu-gui.

"Not really," he answered without looking at her.

"Then you know. Why don't you tell me?"

"Keep your voice down, White Lily," Fu-gui hissed. "You'll find out soon enough."

4

Darkness fell. After the guests had left, the house grew quiet. White Lily sat up in her bed, too excited to sleep. *If only each day were New Year's Day,* she wished. *If only I could be this happy always!*

Silently, her bedroom door opened. Mother hobbled in, holding between her hands a red wooden basin, a wisp of steam clouding above it.

"Mother, what's the hot water for?" White Lily asked as Nai-nai, too, entered the room, a bundle of white bandages tucked under her arm and a low stool in one hand. As her mother put the basin down on the floor, in front of White Lily's bed, tears rolled down her cheeks, like pearls from a broken necklace.

White Lily's cheerfulness evaporated like the steam that hung over the basin. "Mother, is something wrong?"

Nai-nai spoke, her voice quaking hoarsely.

"My dear White Lily, come, come and sit on this stool. It's time ... time ... "

"Time?" White Lily stammered. "Time for what?"

But no one answered. Instead, Mother tenderly pulled off White Lily's socks and guided her feet into the warm water. White Lily stared wide-eyed at the blankness on her mother's face. Her mouth opened and closed but not a word came out. The silence began to frighten her. *It's New Year*, White Lily thought. *So why is Mother weeping, as if somebody died?*

"Don't be afraid," Nai-nai murmured, firmly gripping one of White Lily's legs under her arm. One by one she started folding White Lily's four small toes under, until they pointed along the curve of the sole, until they touched the heel.

"Grandma! That hurts!" White Lily gasped as she tried to pull her leg free. But Nai-nai's hands were too strong. While Nai-nai held White Lily's foot, her mother wrapped the dampened bandage around it, over and over again, ignoring White Lily's screams and heart-rending pleas. It seemed as if both Mother and Nai-nai had suddenly lost their hearing. Nai-nai clasped the struggling girl as Mother wound the cloth around the other foot, turn after turn, to bind White Lily's little toes in that painful and unnatural position. The agony was too much to bear. Finally, White Lily passed out from horror and exhaustion.

Outside, children's laughter and shouts and the sound of their running footsteps floated into the house, amid the explosion of firecrackers that were to chase away the bad luck and misery of the past.

5

When dawn broke, White Lily awoke to find her mother sitting beside her bed, dozing. White Lily groaned. Her feet felt heavy as stones. They ached so!

"Mother, please, please take off the bandages," she begged weakly, reaching for the hated bindings.

"No, no, my dear. I can't. Your father and Nai-nai would never let it happen," Mother whispered sadly, gently pushing White Lily back onto the bed. "The worst part is over, and the pain will go away. Soon you will get used to it, just like Nai-nai and I did. It's the bitterness all females have to eat."

"Not me, Mother!" cried White Lily. "I want my own feet back."

The bandages stayed on. Every passing day White Lily's pain increased as the layers of cloth dried and shrank. They formed bulky, hard shells, like plaster, ruthlessly squeezing her toes against her soles.

There were many visitors. Each of them brought White Lily her favorite candies and cakes and gave out the highest compliments. White Lily pleaded with every one of them to remove the bandages and set her feet free, but embarrassed silence was their only response.

"I'll never run barefoot again," she promised her father. But each time he walked away, his face clouded with fury.

When her future father-in-law got wind of White Lily's complaints and lack of cooperation, he was displeased and muttered that he might have chosen the wrong wife for his son.

White Lily's tears ran dry and her pleas fell on deaf ears. Day after day she watched help-lessly the wrapping and unwrapping of her aching and distorted feet. Now I understand why Mother calls her own feet teardrops, she thought bitterly.

Two months later, White Lily was told that she should try to walk, without assistance. Mother and Fu-gui held her up and watched her make awk-ward steps. Her feet felt like wooden clubs. The pain of each step she took, tottering on her heels and the knuckles of her toes, was like arrows shot into her heart.

"Bound feet are supposed to make you beautiful, and that means a good marriage and a secure future," Mother explained to White Lily. She used herself as an example: wife of a rich landowner and learned official, a glory to her family and ancestors, living a life with no worry about food and clothing.

"Your father's family never would have chosen me as their daughter-in-law if my parents hadn't solemnly promised to have my feet bound. The custom has prevailed for centuries. We women can only obey."

She paused a moment, and went on. "My daughter, your father has heard your cries, but can do nothing to help you either. We must all bow to the old rules and traditions."

Yet Nai-nai pointed out that only the lucky ones were entitled to have "Three-Inch Golden Lilies." Unbound feet were "peasant's feet," she said, and they belonged to the poor. "You don't want to be a worthless girl, do you, Granddaughter?"

"Will Brother Fu-gui have a poor life and an uncertain future?" White Lily asked her father one day as he pored over a ledger in his study. "Why haven't his feet been bound?"

"Stop talking nonsense, you silly girl!" stormed her father, throwing down his writing brush. "How dare you utter such unlucky words against your brother. Fu-gui is a man, and that is his asset. His future lies in his head, not in the size of his feet. He's going to be a scholar, an intellectual like me, governing those who labor with their hands."

"Then, why can't I become a scholar, Father? Why can't you send me to school to learn to read and — ?"

Before she finished her sentence, her father shooed her out of the room.

6

Fu-gui was four years older than White Lily, and a bright student. He loved his sister dearly. During the past weeks, White Lily's every cry of pain and every appeal for help had ripped his heart to pieces. Each time he begged his father's mercy to set his sister's feet free, he was harshly criticized and punished with excessive homework. One evening while studying in his room, he put down his book and went to his father's study once again. There he made a solemn vow to his father: He would look after his sister for the rest of her life if only he could take off the cruel binding from her feet.

"She doesn't need to marry the merchant's son, or anyone else if that's what concerns you, Father. I will take care of her to the very end," he swore.

If it were not for Nai-nai's intercession and Mother's firm reminder that Fu-gui was their only son, Fu-gui would have been sent away to the Imperial Army for contradicting and disobeying his father.

Meanwhile, during her many sleepless nights, White Lily thought over her father's words again and again until they spun around in her head. She gazed at the ceiling for hours in the darkness, wishing with her whole heart that she could find a solution, or a miracle.

One morning, when the first light gilded the top of the willow tree, a thought landed in her mind. Later, while walking stiffly on a paddy dike, holding Fu-gui's arm for support, she told him her idea.

That evening, according to the plan she and Fu-gui had worked out, White Lily made a solemn pledge to Nai-nai, her mother, and her father. She would cause them no further trouble, she promised. She would no longer loosen or unwrap the bandages as she had done whenever she had a chance. She assured them that she had finally come to accept her bound feet. "The rice has been cooked," she quoted her father's saying. "And I also promise to bathe and rebind my feet by myself."

Nai-nai and Father happily agreed, with great relief. But Mother, who knew White Lily best, wondered.

❱

White Lily's compliance brought back the usual peacefulness to the Lee household and regained the satisfaction and approval of the merchant.

7

If Fu-gui had been praised as an obedient and dutiful son by the villagers, he was admired more nowadays as a caring big brother. When White Lily was able to walk on her own, she was frequently seen hobbling around the village with Fu-gui at her side, like an inseparable shadow. Sometimes they traversed the paddy dikes; at others they lingered by the lily ponds. They always ended their daily walks at the riverbank, where they would sit and while away the rest of the afternoon, continuing their seemingly endless conversations. When one pair of lips ceased moving, the other pair went on. They would trail their fingers in the loose black sand, up and down, left and right, sometimes rapidly, sometimes snail-like, as if in slow motion. Anyone who approached them closely enough would see the brother and sister locked in a game of "Xs and Os." But after the curious villager passed by, the game was swept from the sand, and the fingers danced again.

Spring's blossoms burst forth and drifted away on the breeze. The stove-heat of summer came and went, and another lily season passed, making way for the chilly rains of autumn. As New Year approached, White Lily looked forward to her "eighth birthday." For nearly two years now, ever since she had made her promise, White Lily had looked after wrapping, unwrapping, soaking, and oiling her feet on her own. Nai-nai had warned her many times of the grave consequences if the bindings were not carefully maintained: not only would all her pain and misery have been wasted, she would live in sorrow and regret for the rest of her life. "By then no tears, even as much as heaven can hold, will reduce the size of your feet."

Father and Nai-nai were so pleased with White Lily's diligence that they chose not to point out that her feet appeared too thickly bandaged. Her insteps, mounded like two small, round hills, seemed to grow plumper as each month passed. Mother watched her daughter closely, but she kept her doubts to herself.

≈

The family was preparing a grand festivity for this New Year because White Lily's father would turn forty. Tradition dictated that if there was no great celebration on a man's fortieth birthday, he would have no future prosperity. Consequently, the Lee family and their guests enjoyed a lavish dinner that went on for hours, and afterward, the detonations of fireworks echoed inside the courtyard and up and down the alleyways. Across the village, small fire-crackers, hung in long strings from the tips of bamboo poles, popped and crackled in the dark sky. The festivities went on late into the evening.

White Lily and Fu-gui joined the celebration, anxiously yet fearfully waiting to make their own explosion.

8

Next morning, after a festive breakfast of steamed sticky-rice cakes molded into animal shapes, and boiled round dumplings stuffed fat with sweet red bean paste, Father, Nai-nai, Mother, and the merchant and his wife, along with other guests — officials and landlords from the neighboring villages — retired to the sitting room. Fu-gui, the heir of Master Lee, joined them.

After tea was served and more sweets were passed around, Fu-gui whispered quietly, "Father, it's a big day for you. If she may, White Lily has prepared something to wish you a happy birthday."

"Of course, of course," his father agreed, his face bright with pleasure. "Let her in."

Gingerly, White Lily toddled into the room and made a deep bow before her father. Regaining her balance, she announced in a quavering voice, "Father, as my present to you on this remarkable day, I would like to recite a poem

from the Tang Dynasty." Looking straight ahead, she began:

"*Quiet Night Thoughts.*"

White Lily stopped, overwhelmed by the strange stillness around her. She threw a nervous glance at Fu-gui, who raised his eyebrows and beamed from ear to ear.

"*Bright moonbeams glimmer beside my bed*
Like frost on the ground.
Raising my head, I gaze at the moon between
the mountains.
Casting my eyes downward, I miss my old
home town."

Reluctant applause from the guests followed as her last syllable fell. White Lily bowed formally one more time, smiling broadly.

But the merchant and his wife, unhappy with this breach of tradition, scowled at one another. Nai-nai and Mother, their mouths gaping, sat dumbfounded. Everyone's eyes focused on Master Lee, awaiting his reaction to this unusual event.

Master Lee stood up and walked toward White Lily. "Good effort, good effort, my daughter," he said loudly. "You have made that ancient poem sound fresh and interesting."

His words sent a wave of relief through the room. Mother and Nai-nai seemed to relax, White Lily saw from the corners of her eyes. But the merchant and his wife remained stone-faced as they resumed their chat with the guests next to them.

"Father," White Lily said calmly, gathering all of her courage, "I am very grateful for your kind words. Please, if I may, I would like to present to you one more tribute."

An awkward silence fell. Nervous glances were exchanged. Mother, in particular, sat stiffly, her hands clasped tightly on her lap. Master Lee approved with a slight nod and took his seat.

9

Under the watchful eyes of the onlookers, Fu-gui quickly set a small table in the center of the room and placed on it an ink stone, a cup of water, a black ink stick, and a writing brush. He carefully rolled up his right sleeve, wet the stone's surface, and began to rub the ink stick against it. When the ink turned black and thick, White Lily knelt at the table, facing her father, and unrolled a scroll of blank rice paper. Her hand quivered slightly as she picked up the writing brush and dipped its point into the ink. She let out a long, silent sigh before she began to write. Her mouth turned and twisted along with the moving brush, under which each word appeared neat and even: Happy birthday!

"White Lily." Father stood up, attempting to control his astonishment. "This . . . this must have taken years of practice. How . . . ?" For the first time in his service for the dynasty, he found himself

28

unable to finish a sentence in public. Instead, he shot a displeased glance at his wife, who appeared as astounded as her husband.

Nevertheless, White Lily felt encouraged. "Father, I have Brother Fu-gui to thank. You're right. My poor skill didn't come overnight. And here is the proof."

Waiting for no further approval, White Lily reached down and pulled off her shoes. She skill-fully unknotted the cotton strip and loosened the bandages on her feet, releasing a bundle of rice-paper squares that fell to the floor like snowflakes and settled around her feet. On each bit of paper, words had been written, some as big as frogs, others no larger than houseflies.

From the watchers rose *ooohs* and *aaahs* and other expressions of shock and dismay. Nai-nai sat frozen to her seat, hands covering her face in humil-iation. The merchant and his wife, shaking with anger, stormed rudely out of the room, setting the paper squares swirling around one more time. Mother looked on, her face blank and unreadable.

"What's happened, my daughter?" Father quickly approached White Lily, his hands clasped behind his back. "Why did you break your own promise after the agony and turmoil we have all gone through? How dare you, at such a young age, go against centuries-old tradition and bring shame to the family and risk your own future?"

Everyone held back their breath and focused their attention on White Lily.

"Father, I beg your forgiveness," White Lily pleaded, remaining on her knees. Meanwhile, the words she had rehearsed many times with her brother for this occasion rushed into her mind. "I don't mean to hurt you, Nai-nai, Mother, or anyone else. All I ask from you is no more than you offer to Brother Fu-gui, and I will return nothing less than you expect from him." She stopped to catch a breath and continued. "Father, I, too, want to be a scholar, and my effort hasn't been in vain. Look."

So saying, White Lily removed the last strip of cloth, revealing to every staring eye her bare feet — her far-too-big feet. They were Three-Inch Golden Lilies no more. Her curved toes had already made a comeback, assuming their natural position. It was obvious that the bulky, "growing" mounds covered by White Lily's shoes for the past two years had been the folded bits of paper on which she had practiced her calligraphy. And in return, the paper squares had provided much needed air and space for her feet to grow.

"Father, please don't be angry at me or Brother Fu-gui. I just want to learn to read and write so that one day I may become like you, a scholar and a respected official in charge of a village, or a successful businessperson like Uncle Merchant, or if I wish, like Nai-nai and Mother, a mother and wife, taking care of a household." So saying, she looked at her mother, who was now trying her hardest not to show the pride she felt for her daughter.

White Lily thought for a moment as she recalled how hard Fu-gui had tried to explain those strange words to her in plain language and how difficult they had appeared for her to speak them properly, let alone keep in her mind. Now the well-rehearsed terms had come out of her mouth quite naturally, as if she herself had originated them. Her eyes brightened as she declared, "Yes, a chance. An opportunity. That's what I want."

Flabbergasted, her father slowly turned and left the room.

10

While fireworks exploded in the velvet-black sky across the village, White Lily and Fu-gui stared at the candlelight gleaming inside their father's study. The guests had departed. Nai-nai and Mother waited restlessly in the sitting room. When one sat down, the other got up, tottering in circles on cramped feet.

Inside the study, Father sat at his desk before an open book, but turned no pages. Every word White Lily had said that morning came back to his mind, bringing memories of the past. He recalled his own youth, when, contrary to *his* father's wishes, he had decided to be a respected scholar. He had studied in secret, deep into the night, to prepare for the Imperial Civil Service Examinations, through which he could win an eminent position in the service of the emperor. And he remembered vividly how he had asked forgiveness from his father when the imperial edict arrived, announcing his success.

His father's anger and disappointment had tasted bitter in his mouth. But before the day had ended, understanding had prevailed, and finally his father had given voice to his pride in his son. Master Lee felt dampness in his eyes as he thought about White Lily, who dared to challenge the rules under much harsher conditions than his, secretly learning to read and write.

There was a soft tap at the door. Fu-gui came in, followed by White Lily. "Father, I am older and I am responsible for everything that has happened," Fu-gui murmured, kneeling in front of his father. "But times are changing and old rules are giving way to new ones as you yourself have taught me." Taking his father's silence for approval, he went on. "Last week in the village market I saw two men who had cut off their pigtails, defying the law. Yet they were

33

not bothered by the soldiers. I also heard at school that people are questioning some old traditions in posters pasted on walls all over the country."

White Lily, kneeling side by side with Fu-gui, marveled at her brother's eloquence. She watched as her father stood and looked down at Fu-gui with emotion.

"Son, I have thought this matter over. I am proud of you for what you and your sister have done." He then turned to White Lily, his voice softened. "And I am particularly proud of you, White Lily. Yes, let your feet be free and your mind too."

"Father," White Lily quickly jumped to her feet, her eyes sparkling, "are you saying . . ?" She stopped, pressed her lips together as if trying to weigh the rest of the words before they were let out.

Her father smiled.

"Yes, White Lily," Fu-gui interrupted, "you are going . . . " But before her brother completed his sentence, White Lily dashed out of the study and charged into the sitting room where Mother and Nai-nai watched her wide-eyed, unable to believe what they saw.

"Mother, Nai-nai," the cheerful girl burst out, "Father said that I am going to school to learn to read and write."

Nai-nai mumbled, sadly shaking her head.

"I have never heard such a thing in my whole life. You can't possibly —"

"Yes, you can," Mother said firmly as she stood up and held White Lily in her arms. "My daughter, I am so happy for you. I wish I had had your courage when I was your age."

"Mother, you *do* have courage. No other mothers would have done what you did for me. I knew it all along," White Lily whispered.

With her mother and Nai-nai each placing a hand on one of White Lily's shoulders for support, the three of them made their way to the courtyard. They stopped in front of the lily pond, where White Lily took a deep breath before she looked up at the clear evening sky. She shouted, the hardest she ever did: "I am free! I am going to school with my brother, Fugui!" Her ringing voice traveled over the rice paddies, across lily ponds and canals, and into the distance. It was even louder than the blasts of the firecrackers.

Afterword

Legend says that the custom of binding women's feet started during the Tang Dynasty (618–907). A concubine who danced in front of the emperor swirled around on feet that were wrapped tightly with strips of silk cloth. Her graceful steps, light as feathers and swift as clouds, were attributed to her bound feet. She gave such pleasure to the emperor that other women began to bind their feet. The practice became widespread during the Song Dynasty (960–1279). By the Ming era (1368–1644), foot-binding was the norm, especially among women of "good family." In fact, some feudal rulers issued decrees against unbinding.

The process began when a girl was four or five years old, before the bones of her feet were fully formed. Her four small toes had to be bent under and against the sole of the foot; her big toe was also folded in. The foot was then tightly wrapped with strips of cloth to hold the toes in place, at the same time to prevent the foot from growing. By all accounts, the pain was constant and excruciating, lasting for years as the girl matured, and continuing to give discomfort all her life.

The misshapen feet were called "golden lilies" by the Chinese. "Three-inch feet" (about ten centimeters) were a sign of subordination and considered a mark of a woman's beauty. The smaller the pointed feet were, the better. Of course, "golden lilies" were also a symbol of caste, showing a woman's social class.

Not only were her feet distorted, the woman could not walk normally. Her walk was very slow and awkward; her legs were bowed, her feet pointed outward. Therefore, she had to stay in or near her home.

Although opposition to the custom swelled with the revolutions of 1911 and 1919, not until the Liberation in 1949, when the communists took power, was foot-binding abolished.

My story takes place in the Qing Dynasty (1644–1911), the last imperial kingdom in Chinese history, which produced ten emperors in nine generations over 267 years.

White Lily may have escaped the suffering, but many women did not. And one of them was my Great-Aunt Phoenix Sister, whose memory accompanied me as I was creating the story.

WHITE LILY

I was brought up mainly by Great-Aunt. In spite of her so-called "quality of appearance" and her bound feet, she didn't have a "good marriage and secure future," as was predicted when she begged her parents to take off the painful bandages. Instead, after her two failed arranged marriages, Great-Aunt was cast out of her family and village, and ended up living with my family as an "old maid" at the age of twenty-three.

Great-Aunt never once called her bound feet "Three-Inch Golden Lilies" or "Teardrops." As a little girl I called them "Ginger-roots" instead, because that was how they appeared to me: wrinkled and twisted, and often giving off an unpleasant smell. I recall many nights when, before going to bed, I watched Great-Aunt soak her tired feet in a wooden basin. On many occasions, I sat with her in total silence because that was what she preferred. She ignored my curiosity and my many whys.

When I was older, I was able to help her. On cold winter nights, for instance, I would bring her a thermos bottle or add hot water to the basin to keep her feet warm. Yet when sweltering summer nights arrived in Shanghai, when the temperature stayed above 90 degrees Fahrenheit, the soaking of her feet became a miserable ordeal. I would then, holding an oversized banana leaf in each of my hands, fan Great-Aunt as she tended to her feet.

Soaking was essential, Great-Aunt explained to me. The softened feet would make her task a bit easier: trimming off the old skin around her heels and clipping ingrown toenails. Since she walked on her heels, partially supported by her four bent-under toes, her moving around produced a remarkable pounding on the wooden floor in our apartment. My family lived on the second level, and the neighbors below told us they were able to trace the whereabouts of Great-Aunt when she was at home. But they never made any fuss about the thumping over their heads.

How I wish that Great-Aunt were still alive so she would know that I, after all these years, wrote a story about bound feet, telling of the suffering and misery she and many women endured. But most of all, telling of a girl in her time who won her freedom.

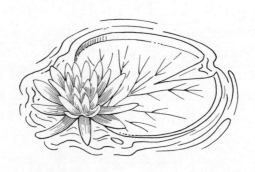

Author's note

"Nai-nai" is "grandmother" on the paternal side: "ai" pronounced as "eye"; Fu-gui, pronounced *Foo-gway* ("ui" as in "away"), means "rich and precious."